MY RIDE OR DIE CHICK

MY RIDE OR DIE CHICK

LIFE OF A CHI-TOWN HUSTLER

SAND DE

To order additional copies of this book, contact:
Xlibris LLC
1-888-795-4274
www.Xlibris.com
Orders@Xlibris.com
551538

CONTENTS

PROLOGUE

This is the story of two young female hustlers, Teenah and Staci, who are both from the Chicago Metropolitan area. We witness them struggle through many of their trials and tribulations. We observe Teenah and Staci being dragged through hell and back. We watch them dust themselves off and survive this thing that we call life!

Urban Dictionary

Bitch: [bich] noun

A confident, attractive woman that doesn't take anyone's shit

Chi: [shy] noun

The Town of Chicago

G: [gee] noun

A title of endearment

Ride or die chick: [ride or die chic] noun

A female who is willing to stick with you even if death is the ultimate fate of their relationship

CHAPTER ONE

THE BETRAYAL

This bitch right here! I fucking can't believe she'd do me like this: fuck my man in my bed. The bed my ass paid for! She knows that I used to change my men like I change my draws. She's seeing me, allowing Captain Fuck-a-Hoe to hang around me and my shorties for these past two and a half years, nobody meets my precious children! And this grimy, thirsty, dirty-ass muthafucker gonna go and fuck my bitch, my G, my ride or die chick in our crib, the one that I built for my little and most beautiful family! His ole thirsty ass! He knows that she was the one and only bitch that I fucks with on real basis. Of all of the bitches to fuck, he chose to fuck, my G, my bitch, my ride or die chick. After all me and my G have been through, all of our ups and downs, relationships, ass whippings, miscarriages, other bitches, and all types of bullshit, now he go and pull this shit, this BULLSHIT! Hell, somebody has to die, and die right fucking now! Then I thought, *Before I kill you both, I want to know why and how you could do this to me.*

I should've known something was up when we'd all get together and he would always start a fight with her every muthafuckin' time. I would just dismiss it as two separate strong-willed personalities competing for my attention. They'd get into it like two starving dogs fighting over one small bowl of gourmet dog food. He'd pick with her over the simplest—and I mean the most simplest—things. He'd fuck with her about where she parked in the big-ass driveway; no matter where she parked, it would be in his way. When she'd come over to the crib, why does she always gotta come over here? Why can't she ever stay at her own crib? When I go and chill at her crib, he's always asking, "What time are you gonna be home? Why you with that bitch? Why do you always, always kick it over to her crib? Why can't y'all ever kick it at yo spot?" He was a hot-ass mess! He'd act worst than a muthafucking three-year-old spoiled brat throwing a muthafucking temper tantrum!

In-fucking-credible!

I pulled up and spotted Staci's snow-white 2012 Jaguar XJ series laced with peanut-butter-colored baby-soft monogramed Italian leather seats, sporting personalized plates, slightly hidden and parked off to the side of my two-and-a-half car garage and still resting in my driveway! I pulled my car into my driveway and parked next to Larry's black-on-black 2010 Cadillac Escalade ESV sitting on twenty-four-inch chromed-out split five-star rims laced with low-profile tires!

I heard the Isley Brothers' "Voyage to Atlantis" blaring way outside in the driveway. Ron Isley's sexy ass voice was cascading down from the second-floor balcony, where my five hundred-square-foot bedroom is located! I noticed the red light peeking through the vertical blinds as if the light was a convict attempting to elope from Alcatraz Island in the middle of the night!

I entered my home through the kitchen entrance; I slipped off my six-inch open-toed leopard print House of Deréon stilettos so that I could stealthily move across my marble kitchen floor undetected. I quietly and gracefully passed my solid granite island and countertops perched atop of cherry oak cabinets. Next, I passed by the stairwell in the kitchen, and I head up to the quieter set of stairs in the hallway adjacent to the family room. Once I reached the split three-tier staircase, I flowed to the right staircase, which would allow me to go undetected for a few more minutes. As I begin to ascend up the solid cherry oak staircase, I press my back firmly against my smoked lilac walls while maneuvering around my fine artwork, like I was a very well-trained Navy SEAL on a top-secret special ops mission. I reached the summit of my mountainous staircase; I am forced to pause for a hot second just to catch my breath from anxiety, anticipation, and exhaustion. I'm at the mouth of my hallway; there's no turning back now! Bitch, let's go and bust these dirty-ass, back-stabbing muthafuckas. I take a huge breath; now I'm listening for moans and other sex sounds creeping from my bedroom.

With a feverish pace, I stealthily strolled down my dimly lit corridor toward Armageddon and the melodic voice of Ronald Isley, which was escaping behind my huge bedroom doors. My corridor appeared to look as though it was the art museum located on Wabash Avenue in downtown Chicago. My hallways played second fiddle only to Le Louvre over in France, with works of art from world-famous artist, such as Michelangelo, Claude Monet, and Vincent van Gogh, draped along them!

I finally reach my destination, my beautiful bedroom and the well-constructed twelve-foot towering solid cherry oak double doors that are garnishing my room. I'm still hearing the soulful sounds of Ronald Isley and the Isley Brothers that are blaring from the other side of the doors: "Can I go on my way without you?" Those are the same sentiments that were racing through my mind about my G, my bitch, my ride or die chick. I push open the heavy-ass doors, and this thirsty bitch is beating his big black shiny dick with his feet propped up on my dark-chocolate, butter-soft La-Z-Boy chair. My G, my bitch, my ride or die chick is heavily oiled up and is standing on my California king-size sleigh bed, wearing nothing but her black Italian-made lace Claudia Lemes bra with the sexy-ass matching black Italian lace boy shorts, swaying to the music as if she's working over in the underground at the world-famous magic city of Atlanta! What the fuck!

Larry yanked his head around as if he was on a roller coaster at Great America. Larry started gripping! He said, "Hey, darling," in a way that Larry would only say it as if there are seven A's in darling! "Wh-wh-what you doing home? You are supposed to be on the plane on yo way out of town to the West Coast!"

So I asked him, "Is this what happens every time I leave out of town? Yo muthafucking dirty ass be entertaining all types of other bitches in my muthafucking crib. You couldn't even have the decency to take them hoes to the fucking hotel! Way to go, Larry! You dirty-ass bastard!"

Chapter Two

THE ENCOUNTER

(FLASHBACK)

The night started out as a typical summer party night. It was early into this particular Friday night; I guess it was around five-ish. Staci hits me up on my hip. "Hey, G, let's hit the Signature Room before we hit up the club!" We love going downtown to get our eat and get our hip-hop on! I took me a hot-ass bubble bath; I damn near boiled my sexy-ass copper-brown skin off this sexy-ass body of mine! I trimmed up Ms. Kitty jus in case somebody gets lucky! I hopped out my tub. Oh shit, it's damn near seven. I'm in rush mode now, but I'm not dressing too damn fast. You just can't rush perfection! I oiled up in my shea-and-cocoa-butter mixture, making damn sure that I hit them heels. Ain't nothing like a bad bitch with fucked-up cracked heels! I dusted a light layer of powder on so I stay nice and dry! I walked out of my precious pink ladies' bathroom and about six steps into my closet to the Fuck 'em dress section of my clothes! I spot that bad fire-engine, red-hot Michael Kors V-neck sleeveless dress that screams classy yet sexy. I slip on my gold Donna Karan wedges and a gold Kleinberg snakeskin belt just for a splash of wow! A few pumps of Trina's Diamond Princess and I'm good to go! Staci picks me up in her fresh to def cool whip! Her white XJ series floated up as if she was in the Ghost.

We hopped onto the Dan Ryan jus south of our hood on 111th, between LA Fitness and Chi-Town's very best barbecue. We rolled north on the Dan Ryan Expressway, clipping along at seventy miles per hour. We noticed the beautiful downtown skyline steadily approaching. We arrived at 875 North Michigan Avenue, the base of the John Hancock Building. We loved to check out the skyline of the Chi, one of America's very best skyline—period! Hell, maybe even the best skyline in the world from sunset until sunup! The skyline after sunset is as beautiful as the national Christmas tree on the White House south lawn during the holiday season!

We walked through the automatic sliding doors. Staci and I proceeded through the beautiful lobby and headed toward the elevator. We entered the semicrowded elevator filled with business executives and other professional-looking people. Up we went to the ninety-fifth floor of the John Hancock Building located on Chicago's magnificent mile. The ride to the ninety-fifth floor was surprisingly quick for that many stories to climb. We reached our destination— the ninety-fifth floor. We were greeted by this sexy, well-groomed Italian maître d'. Michael—I believe he said his name was—seated us in the very intimate dining area with a very gorgeous view showing off Chicago's very beautiful skyline. We marveled on how clear the stunning ten-foot windows were, damn near invisible.

For my appetizer, I ate king crab toast. As a main course, I had their famous surf and turf with the ten-ounce steak on the side. I was served locally grown asparagus with lemon and olive oil. Of course I washed all that beef down with a glass of Rosé Brut wine. Staci ordered the lobster bisque as her appetizer. My G then had the cioppino as her main course; she enjoyed the roasted mushrooms, fresh herbs, brown butter vinaigrette on the side, and a glass of blanc de blanc wine. I passed on the dessert, but my bitch ordered a very tasty-looking raspberry cheesecake garnished with raspberry puree, passion fruit, and fresh berries. Staci claims that it tastes ten times better than it looks. Well, that shit would be too damn good to me then. I'd never stop eating that shit! I'd be like a crackhead trying to get a slice of that fire-ass cheesecake at three in the goddamn morning.

Staci and I headed south on Michigan Avenue, then over to Wabash Avenue. We stopped at the Shrine Nightclub to get our hip-hop on! It was packed up in the joint. There were several local celebrities hanging out, a couple of former and current Chicago

Bulls and Bears players, and several radio personalities getting there sip on. You had a bunch of ballers and wannabe ballers in the club. Niggas dressed to the nine, and the bitches where better dressed than a Hollywood red carpet event. Me and my bitch, my ride or die chick had a muthafucking ball. Hell, we practically lived on the fucking dance floor. We dragged ourselves off the dance floor long enough to swallow a couple coconut Cîroc and pineapples juice for me and red berry Cîroc and cranberry juice for my bitch. Staci spotted an old acquaintance of hers, and we crossed the room to speak to him. As Staci went to introduce me, fine chocolate said in his deep manly voice, "My name is Jeremiah, but my close friends call me Jay!"

"Well, my name is Teenah, and my friends call me Teenah, but you can call me Desert!" We all chuckled!

Me, my bitch, and this double-chocolate tatted-up Adonis looking like a swollen Idris Elba headed over to the Embassy Suites Hotel. This is where he's staying while in the Chi on a business trip. We're listening to a duties CD that I burnt, which is usually in the radio of my whip. Me and my G were sitting here, sipping on some pineapple Cîroc and papaya juice. Jay's double-chocolate ass is sipping on Hennessy XO straight, grown-man style! We were listing to the dusties, getting all hot, horny, and wet! This chocolate Adonis starts rubbing my clit like he was polishing some fine china while my bitch is stroking on his thick dark-chocolate twelve-inch dick. His big-ass dick looking like an extra-large, king-size melting snicker. My bitch jus swallowed all fucking twelve inches of his dark-chocolate joystick. Damn, she's a soldier, no gag, no moaning, no punk, straight like a champion dick sucker! Up and down from the tip of his head down to his pelvis and back up to the tip of his chocolate mushroom. She's rolling her tongue around the head and to the shaft of his big rock-hard black dick. Staci worked that dick as a child would do a Popsicle during a classic heat wave in the middle of July on a steamy Chicago's hot summer day. My bitch is yanking on his fat-ass dick as if she was competing in a tug-of-war with his thick-ass chocolate dick! He remained focused, and he was working my clit with his full lips and soft fingers. Jay moved his snakelike tongue fast, slow, soft, hard, deep, and shallow! Whew, that was a fantastic night!

CHAPTER THREE

HUSTLING BIGG DADDY

Oh yeah, and that time when we beat that old-school hustler from the NYC area for a lil more than forty stacks. We were playing the role of two dumb-ass country gals fresh off the turnip truck! He thought he had found two dumb-ass country hicks and thought we were too damn simple to know that he was fronting, and he was only the middle man for a more powerful and important hustler, Big Slim! Bigg Daddy was too damn proud and embarrassed to admit to his friends and the big boss that two dumb-ass country chicks could beat his fat ass out of forty stacks or more!

We spotted our mark forty-five minutes before we allowed him to find us, these two pitiful ass, helpless dumb hicks! My bitch Staci was going by the name Altheia. I was using the name Addie Lee.

She was rocking her tight ass skittles green Deréon mini-skirt, her six-inch green Christian Louboutin (red bottoms) stilettos. Shei was rocking her extra-tight white see-through, button-down Ecko red blouse; only the three middle buttons were buttoned up!

I was rocking my super-short burnt-orange cheerleader skirt, my knee-high black socks, and burnt-orange patent leather Jimmy Choos. We were all that and some, Shidd. I would've pick us up as fine as we were looking! Damn!

Bigg Daddy, our mark, was roughly standing six three to six four. He weighed about 340–350 pounds, not quite an athletic build but not really fat. He was probably an ex-athlete! Bigg Daddy was balding, sporting a low-cut afro with long salt-and-pepper sideburns. He wore black horn-rimmed, Steven Q. Urkel-style Lauren Bugatti glasses! Always smiling with his yellowish-brown, jagged smoker's teeth as if he's rocking a full set of thirty-two pearly whites. He was wearing a black and red Rocawear jean fit with a pair of black and white python-pattern snakeskin Mauri boots! His left wrist was sparkling with a couple of man-size gold Gucci link bracelets and a beautiful red rock Chrono by Marc Jacobs on his other wrist! Showing a lil taste and rocking jus a little bit of class! Bigg Daddy was in his mid to late fifties (fifty-five to fifty-eight), average looks for an older gentleman nearing his sixties.

Bigg Daddy thought that he had two new woes for the track. We allowed him to think he was teaching us the game while preparing us for his stable, which was really the big boss's stable. Bigg Daddy was jus tending the farm while Big Slim was handling his other more important and more pressing businesses! He was very careless with the combination to the boss man's safe! We waited until Friday night when we were supposed to hit the track before we rocked his whole understanding! Bigg Daddy went to drop off the first four girls—Strawberry, Juicy, China, and Bronze Venus—at their spots. Afterward, he was to return and then drop me, Altheia, Baby Cakes, and Coco off at our spots!

Bigg Daddy would be gone for around seventeen to twenty-three minutes, depending on the traffic lights. Coco saw me dialing the combination to Bigg Daddy's huge old-school black sentry safe. Coco spoke with a very heavy Mediterranean accent. Coco said, "What are chew doing, Mami? Chew betta not be es steeling from papi grande!"

I said "Bitch, grow the fuck up. His fat ass didn't work for this paper. Each one of y'all sucked and fucked for this paper. Y'all don't owe him shit, not a muthafucking thang." I then told her, "Don't stay a simple bitch all yo stupid as life!"

Coco was like, "Chew wait a goddamn minute beech," while pointing her gel-tipped fire-engine red fingers in my face!

Staci jumped up and flipped out her always-ready, razor-sharp switchblade. "Bitch, you don't want none of this. I'm ready to cut me a muthafucka from asshole to appetite. Try it, bitch, try it!"

Man, Althea (I was staying in complete character and keeping my cool) I screamed to Staci, "Althea, let's go. These simple bitches ain't going anywhere and sure as fuck don't want none! I got the chop, let's ride!" We faded into the night with a ten-minute head start on Bigg Daddy. We headed west while Bigg Daddy and his crew were thinking we headed back down south. The joke was on them! We hit them for a damn good lick, bounced! Thanks, NYC!

CHAPTER FOUR

BEVERLY, OUR HOOD

Back on the south side (Wild Wild Hunids), I arrived home earlier than I had originally expected, but my pockets are a whole lot fatter than I thought they'd be! I figured we'd hit a lick for about five stacks, but we grabbed twenty stacks apiece. Damn, what a great week, a straight come up.

I dropped Staci off at her and her daughters, Khadijah and Brooklyn, 3,500-square-foot crib on 110th Street jus east of Longwood Avenue, one of those large-ass brick cribs with a huge backyard and beautiful landscape up front, lovely ass curb appeal! The driveways in her neighborhood are littered with high-end luxury vehicles, both foreign and domestic, nothing costing less than $60 stacks. Long-ass driveway after driveway after driveway of sleek expensive luxury cars. This is a far, far, far cry better neighborhood than the one we grew up in Harvey a.k.a. Harvey-world. Staci was the last-born child of a southern-style Baptist minister. Reverend Johnson had five children, two of which are girls.

I pulled up to my large-ass crib on 101st and Winchester; trees draped across my well-manicured lawn as if I lived in South Beach or somewhere majestic! I see the lawn care service company pulling off as I pull up to my custom two-and-a-half-car unattached garage at the end of my very long driveway! My neighbor, an ex-Chicago Bears linebacker, is outside, washing his 2013 Opel black-on-black Cadillac XTS! The shine on his XTS is shining so damn bright that the bling was blinding me, and I damn near ran into the fucking garage door.

My four-bedroom, three-and-a-half bathroom was definitely enough space for me and my ten-year-old twins, K'tyrra and T'kyrra; my three-hundred-pound English bull mastiff, Jezabelle, the queen of block, a true boss bitch!

My crib is a very beautiful Victorian-style home, something straight out of *Better Homes and Garden* magazine. A lawn that appears as if there's a professional gardener attending to the flowers every day! Growing up on the 4th (187 west 154th Street), we had no flowers, no gardens, no grass, and no nothing! So as a mother, I teach my twins how to garden! So I'm out with the twins three times a week, teaching them how to care for a flower bed without using chemicals and earth-harming pesticides. The twins enjoy learning how to respect the earth and help improve their small corner of the earth! K'tyrra, the elder twin, is a better gardener. She has a beautiful green thumb. T'kyrra, a whole six minutes younger, handles Jezabelle much better than her six-minute-older big sister. The twins are so much alike yet so much different! K'tyrra loves purple, yet T'kyrra will kill for anything green! TK is a wonderful musician, and KT is a Juilliard-bound dancer!

K'tyrra is all about concrete and numbers, yet her younger sister is a huge dreamer who dreams of foreign places and foreign lands. They are my girls, my soul, my only reason for living!

Staci's two girls are Khadijah, and Brooklyn. Ms. Khadijah is eight years old, and Ms. Brooklyn, Bee, as we usually call her, a hot mess, is seven going on forty. Bee's a very r-e-s-p-e-c-tful yet growner than that thang, lil lady. Girlfriend be rocking purses everywhere she goes. Her swag is way off the swag meter, just a little boss-type lady. Now Khadijah, on the other hand, is Bee's polar opposite, a straight athlete. Khadijah, or Dijah, as we affectionately call her, will choose Jordans over heels any day, every day, and all day.

Staci be running from beauty pageants to AAU games all week long, nonstop! Most of the times, they're on different days; but occasionally, we have to haul one of her girls—my nieces, as we like to label each other's girls—to one of their events. Anything for the little princesses! No, don't get it twisted; she does a whole hell of a lot for my little woman as well! It is a very fair trade-off of different tasks and chores for each other's girls. We are constantly teaching them culture and skills so that the girls don't have to grind like we did!

CHAPTER FIVE

PHONE FUN

My bitch had been working at the phone sex company for about three months or so; that bitch just kept bragging on how much chop she's making off all these lonely and miserable old fucks. My G introduced me to her boss, one of the coldest bitches in the Chi with the best mouth pieces that you'll ever hear. That is until I open my sexy mouth and you hear me start talking my shit! bad, bad bitch! She works at the Lonely Night's Companion Company, stacking paper like the Federal Reserve Bank, singing, "I got stacks to the ceiling!"

So I'm at The J-O-B and this phone call comes through. "Welcome to Lonely Nights. Hello, operator 3425. How can I be yo companion tonight?"

Caller: Hell-hello,

Me: Hello, Bigg Daddy, can I call you Bigg Daddy?

Caller: Don't fucking hustle me. I know how this shit go! Flat fee $35 first ten minutes and $5 a minute for next hour, then $2.50 for the rest of the time.

Me: I'm sorry, Bigg Daddy. Sorry, sir, what do you want me to call you?

Caller: You jus call me C!

He stopped abruptly as if he was a teenager and he's mother walked in the room while he was having phone sex. LOL!

Caller: Cecil! Cecil J Jones. Yeah, Cecil Jones!
Me: Okay, Cecil. What can I do for you?
Cecil: I just want to talk. I don't want or need for you to make me feel good.
Me: Okay, Cecil, let me hear what you got!
Cecil: I'm a bad man, a bad, bad man! Wait, hold the fuck up. How do I know that I can trust you?
Me: Baby, whatever you say, I'm keeping to myself.
Cecil: It don't fucking matter.
Me: Okay, baby, I'm here. I'm all ears.
Cecil: Like I said, I'm a bad, bad man. I've killed a man once before, just for saying my name in public. I've sold millions of millions of dollars of dope. I've pimped runaway teenage girls. I have several politicians, judges, chiefs of police, and so-called important dignitaries on my payroll. I've done every damn thing that is illegal up under the sun that you can possibly imagine, and at the end of the day, I enjoy laying up with a sexy as thug. Yeah, that's right, I enjoy the intimate company of a man every night!

I sit there quiet as a church mouse with my damn mouth wide open in udder fucking shock! You could've flew a passenger airplane into my muthafucking big-ass mouth. What the fuck! This went on for several weeks. Cecil would call every Thursday, around eleven thirty at night, and would request to speak to operator 3425; and in detail, he'd describe his different sexual escapades. Some of his shit would be *way* out there. I'd be like, *Wow, what the fuck!* to myself, of course. I never judged him, and I just allowed him to get all this wild shit up and off of his chest. Sometimes he would be crying at the end of our phone call. He'd end each phone call the same way every time he'd say, "All right, precious, I'll be to see you again next week in the same spot in the same corner at the same time!"

I would say the exact same thing to him as well, "All right, sweetie, I'll be wearing that same red dress that you are so crazy about." We would laugh, knowing I'm not what he crave.

I truly enjoyed coming to work, talking mad shit to all of these horny as old men wasting their pensions and kids' collage trust funds. When Cecil Day would roll around, I would get very hyped to come to work just to hear Cecil's stories. Instead of saying TGIF, I'd say TGIT, thank God it's Thursday! Eleven thirty could not get here fast enough on Thursdays.

CHAPTER SIX

BOBO AND THE BEAST

Remembering the time Staci was in a very abusive relationship with that sorry-ass woman-beating ass nigga from the Swamp, Altgald Gardens, block 2, if I remember correctly. Emmm, his name was Bobo, I do believe. Bobo was a very dark chocolate well-built brother as if he worked out sixteen hours a day every single day of the week. Bobo was rocking those long ass hip-hop dreads. Always rocking Jordans, or Air Force Ones, and True Religion jean fits. A typical Altgald Garden's hustler, getting his paper on, grabbing all of that Arab money! A triple-hitter type of nigga, serving that kush, cain (cooked and raw), and that heroin! Just killing the whole game. He was like second in command with the GD's before his little accident over on Doty Road! He used to keep his foot knee deep up in Staci's ass. His last epic ass whopping placed her in LC of M's Hospital for five weeks, two of which she spent in ICU having a miscarriage. Staci's third miscarriage with Bobo's punk ass! I picked her up from the hospital because his sorry ass wouldn't even pick her up from the hospital, but he sure as hell was at her house half of an hour later trying to get some pussy. His dog ass didn't care about her well-being, nope, not for one single solitary minute! Luckily, her girls where at her mom's crib, Granny Pearl, for that week that he fucked her up!

The girls stayed with me while Staci was in the hospital and in the following month, while my home girl, my sister, recovered, so that the girls could continue attending practice and their weekly scheduled activities.

Once the winds died down about her epic ass whopping and people kinda forgot about this last past episode, we began plotting on Bobo's demise. Our minds were racing: What kind of death this fucking bastard deserves? A bullet is way too muthafucking fast, and that bogus bitch was not worth the $2 for the cost for each bullet. Even though I I'd love to shoot his bitch ass with my nickel-plated Nina Taurus, right in his cold heart.

It's Friday night, midsummer, and all the drivers are starting to line their dragsters, hot rods, and muscle cars on 130th, just west of Doty Road. They were prepping their cars, talking shit among each other, placing bets, and getting psyched for their runs at race perfection. Bobo's routine was the same every Friday night; he'd hit the Factory (a local strip joint on Doty Road), roll his all black custom metal flake 2002 Lincoln Blackwood, Harley Davison edition sitting on twenty-two-inch chromed-out triblade choppers, towing his candy apple-red 1978 modified Buick Regal with a super charged five-hundred-cubic-inch 1970-something Cadillac motor. Whatever all that shit mean, he said it enough when he'd refer to his car (the Beast). Bobo would pull his blackwood up to about one hundred feet from 130th on Doty Road, crank his loud-ass regal up, and then roll it off the trailer then he would burn rubber going backward about twenty-five feet, then Bobo would pull the beast around the Blackwood. The beast would briefly run down Doty Road, briefly stopping at the stop sign and proceed to the check point on 130th. Bo would place his typical bet of ten stacks near the finish line where C-fluid and the other ballers would handle their business transactions. C-fluid is the boss of Chicago's underworld, and no one makes money without 10 percent of the proceeds coming through C-fluid's hands.

This week would be a little different; he rolled the beast off of the trailer, gunned the beast in reverse, as usual, his tiers screeching like gigantic bald eagles. Bobo dropped the regal into drive. They went speeding off, but this time, he didn't stop, or shall I say couldn't stop. Up the ramp they went and across 130th. Now Bobo and the Beast went careening nose first off of the bridge of 130th and onto the railroad tracks several feet west of the Bishop Ford Expressway. Boom! A great ball of flames went the Beast and Bobo! RIP, Beast, and fuck you, Bobo. Your sorry ass won't be missed! You sorry ass bastard!

I guess it is true what they say: Revenge is a dish best served cold. I felt very sorry that his mother had to bury her third child. I'm not sorry nor remorseful that he had to die though!

Chapter Seven

THE LAKEFRONT

Staci, I, and a couple of bitches from TTHS, our alma mater, were kicking it in the old hood (Harvey-world). We were sitting back, sipping on us some Corona Lights, blowing back that Afghan, just reminiscing about our old high school days, or shall I say daze! One of these smart bitches (sarcastically spoken) suggested that we go down to the Lakefront. Stacy R. wanted to roll to the South Shore Country Club. Re-re's ole ghetto ass wanted to hit hood ass, Rainbow Beach, then Keesha was like, "Let's go to Thirty-fifth Street beach. Y'all know it's the shit now since they remodeled the spot!"

Everybody was like, "Yeah, hell yeah, let's do this, bitches!"

Stacy R., cool as hell and laid back, don't fuck with anybody, but you better not piss that bitch off! She will go ham on a muthafucka in a fucking heartbeat and wouldn't give two fucks on who the hell you are! And this bitch has the nerve to be a fucking professional. This wild-ass bitch is a fucking accountant, a goddamn CPA, and the fucking president of her company.

Re-re, a beast girlfriend, is from the darkest part of hell. Nobody but nobody fucked with Re-re growing up or as a fucking adult. She's a real woman, but this bitch acts and fights like a fucking man!

Here's the funniest part of the joke: Re-re owns and operates a day care center. She's a true Dr. Jekyll, and Mrs. Hyde type of muthafucka. How could someone be so ghetto and rugged but be sensitive and sweet with the babies? The babies just adore her ass too.

Keesha, this bitch gets it in with the very best of them. You had better not let her blind ass get into the driver's seat, though. This bitch can't see shit past the damn hood ornament but always wanna grab somebody's steering wheel. Nawh, bitch, scoot the fuck over, with yo blind ass! Now Keesha is an LPN and a Sunday school teacher. Go figure! I guess for all of the ass that she has kicked growing up, she gotta find some kind of way to get into heaven.

Me, the owner of my very own upscale hair salon, the Lady's Palace! Over at the Lady's Palace, you could get your hair and nails done, facial, and complete full body massage. My full service shop is located in the Beverly Area on 103rd and Western Avenue.

Staci is a business major who works as an office manager downtown in the Mercantile Mart with one of the leading Fortune 500 companies. When Staci goes on vacation, she is required to bring her Blackberry with her so they can have her walk them through difficult and tough problems that her company is struggling on.

We all mob up in Stacy R.'s whip; she has the most room out of all of us. Just like routine Keesha's blind ass say I'm driving! We all say at the same time as if we are a quartet. No, bitch, get yo ass in the back. We all giggle, even Keesha's blind ass! Stacy R. tells her to get her ass all the way in the back! Stacy R. is pushing a full-size SUV, a big boy's toy! Stacy owns a moonlight white Infiniti QX56 with wheat and mocha leather interior. This bitch is rolling around in a fucking apartment building on wheels, just a big dumb-ass muthafucking SUV. Stacy R. swears that it costs her around $ 125 to fuel that apartment building on wheels up if she allows that big bitch to get all the way on empty. Every time her truck gets on a half of a tank, she's pumping that liquid gold into her tank.

We were rolling down the Fourth (154th Street) in great disbelief on how ragged and fucked up that the once-beautiful downtown Harvey has gotten. All of the once-beautiful buildings and rows upon rows of businesses are gone, all gone away. The Fourth has been reduced to abandoned, dilapidated, and boarded condemned piles of rubble. The Fourth was once home of five drugstores with the names such as Oliver Rexal's, Regal's, and Community Drugs and other prestigious and important-sounding family names!

We continue west toward Dixie Highway; we pass by the raggedy-ass tan project-looking buildings behind the day care, which was a former drugstore from way back in the days! We reach the old Burger King, which is now a Payday Loan Store, and we turn north on Dixie, passing by more destitute and despair! The apartment building on wheels cruise by the vacant lot that used to be the first mall in the south suburb, Dixie Square Mall, then known as the mall that the Blues Brothers ransacked with their decommissioned police car. We pass by the Harvey Police Station on one side and dilapidated piles of rubble head toward Sibley Boulevard and the Sibley Entrance of the I-57. We are rolling pass a rather mundane gas station, after a church and a liquor store and crackhead-filled rotten buildings. We reach Sibley; we debate if we should stop by the new-wave-style building of Mickey D's or hit the Dunkin' Donuts resting across the street that was an old car lot way back in days. We pass on both as we decided we'd pick up something in the city. We hop on at Sibley, and we merge onto northbound I-57. We are rolling hard and blowing back even harder. Lakefront, here we come, five of the baddest bitches that you'll ever see at one time.

We get down to the Lakefront, chilling, enjoying ourselves, listening to Chrissette Michelle's banging-ass CD, just passing dat Afghan around her apartment on fucking wheels, getting good, real good! So we hop out of the QX56. We here Chief Keefe blaring in the air "That's the Shit I Don't Like." We filling ourselves and dis Chief Keefe nigga! We bobbing and swinging to his dope heat, fist pumping and all, just kicking it hard! We posturing like we on stage at the Regal Theater, throwing our own fucking concert! Then from nowhere, this hoods-ass dude walks up on us, followed by three other insignificant thug-looking late-teenage boys, maybe early twenties, no more than twenty-one or twenty-two, just talking shit, nothing too special about them or the conversation. All of a sudden, these four gutter ass bitches roll up on us, talking loudly but really not saying too damn much! I guess them niggas where with them tired-ass bitches or something.

We don't know, really didn't care. All I know is these raggedy-ass bitches were blowing my fucking high! What the fuck! Bag up off me, bitch. All of a sudden, I'm nose to nose with this halitosis-breath-heaving heifer! Her breath smelled like her teeth were having a gang fight up in her mouth, and by the looks of it, the raggedy teeth were winning! One of her girls pushed me, and I fall to the ground. Whew (large exhale)! Why in the fuck did she do that? Before I could even get up to my feet, my G, my bitch, Staci, bust that bitch upside her goddamn head with one of them damn Corona Light bottles. That bitch's blood was every fucking where. Re-re, fast, heavy handed as done, cold knocked one of the niggas out and was already squaring up with another one. Keesha was instantly stumping the short funny-looking bitch when I was like, "Let's ride, bitches, before we get our ass locked the fuck up." Before we break to the apartment on wheels, I stump ole raggedy mouth in her already ugly-ass face. We all hop in and start laughing our asses off, talking like juveniles about what everyone else did in our quick little mala with these simple-minded projects motherfuckas. That shit was way too funny.

Chapter Eight

TRAPPED IN THE PROJECTS

In one of my roughest situations that I had to deal with in my life, my G was there to help me through it. Wow, wow, wow, what memories, the time that I really needed my sister there for me was after I was kidnapped and repeatedly raped by these three high niggas tripping off them X pills. We called people who was high off X pills rollers. I can honestly say rollers were very dangerous individuals. The biggest misconception about X pills is that they bring you to a great euphoria. Actually, they enhance whatever mood that you are in, so if you are horny, you will be horny times a hundred. However, if you are pissed, you are pissed times a hundred, and that is a major recipe for disaster.

I was held over in the new projects up in dirty-ass Robbins. I'm knowing that I shouldn't went to the Blue Room all by myself, but I was gone off that 1800 coconut, sweet but deadly! These three dirty-ass undercover fags had me trapped in a roach-infested, trashed-filled, smelly ass apartment. The apartment smelled as if someone changed diapers for about a week straight and just tossed them onto the motherfucking floor. I was simply hoping to die, then to spend another fucking moment in this nasty-ass garbage and roach-infested hellhole. These three crazy-ass rollers would take turns jumping up and down on me. The three rollers went by the names Blaq, Jo-jo, and

Killa. Blaq was 6'4", 195 pounds. He was an ex-basketball star from Old Main who turned to a wannabe hustler. He looked as if he could or should be running point guard for somebody's NBA team. This pussy-ass bottom feeder would whip his ten-inch extra-thick black-ass dick out and fuck me in my ass every single goddamn time he'd show up. This thirsty bitch wouldn't even grease me up either. His sole intent and purpose was to bring me pain, extreme pain at that! The last time he raped me, I begged and begged him to use some lube of some kind. This undercover fag spit onto my asshole, then fucked me even harder. It felt as if my asshole was on fire while he was trying to push my colon up through my mouth. I just couldn't take it anymore. My mind took me back to a much, much more happier place and time in my life; it was my six-year-old birthday party. This is one of my fondest moments and memories of my mommy and daddy; they were just showering me with all of their love. This day was all about me, Little Ms. Teenah. Everyone here was here just to see Lil Teenah. I had received about a million gifts on my day. Everyone showed up with gift in their hands, and they were all for me and only me, Lil Ms. Teenah. I was the princess for the day.

"Oh shit, what the fuck!" I'm forced back into reality by the succulent smoke from Blanche's barbeque house, and the stale shit smell of this fucked-up apartment pissed the fuck off at myself. *Bitch, what the fuck are you doing?* I fuss at myself, in my head of course. *You're being gang raped, and you're cuming, hard as hell too! Bitch, why would you cum? How could you cum, bitch? You are not enjoying this fucked-up shit. How in the world can I disrespect myself like this and cum? You betrayed yourself!* Now I'm lying there all numb inside, in major disbelief that I could do such a god-awful thing to myself. Father God, can I please jus die right now? Please end my suffering and take me now!

Jo-jo, the next bastard, was about 6'0", 210 pounds, an Allen B. Shepard dropout who thought that school was too slow for him. Every time Jo-jo's simple nickel slick-ass would come around, he'd have a brand-new scam. He'd never pass up an opportunity to beat someone out of their chop. Just plain thirsty with it. Jo-jo would ask me, "You like this? You like this dick, bitch, don't yo?" Then he'd say, "This dick good to you, ain't it? Hey, bitch, I'm talking to you!" I would never answer him; I would not moan. Hell, I would not even cry. I was not gonna give him the satisfaction of even knowing if he was hurting me or not. I would check out mentally for the whole five minutes that he would be up on top of me jumping up and down, looking like a muthafucking overgrown-ass rat, just cheesing while his breath was burning the hair in my nose. His breath smelled like OE and shit turds all mixed together.

Then there is Killa, a 6'1", 255 pounds ex-Robbins Eagle, who couldn't find success in high school football that followed him throughout his little league football career! He's the type of nigga that's always talking about that great game or great season where he put up superhero, untouchable type of numbers (everyone kept repeating these bullshit about this bastard and his past) like he's someone of importance! He's nothing but a sorry-ass failure living in the past of his own glory. What little and very limited success that there was! When Killa was jumping up and down on me, he would want me to look him into his cold, dark, and steely, beady eyes. I would look him in his sad pitiful eyes while he was jumping up and down on me. He'd get mad and slap me a couple of times, but I'd never give in to his demands. After he'd smack me five or six times as if he was trying to realign my jaw, I'd be in my happy place, he'd be jumping up and down on a lifeless body, a corpse for all that mattered. He'd eventually get frustrated, hop up off of me, and jag off until he'd bust a good nut, which was usually onto my body. Then the punk-ass, undercover fag would laugh and smear his extra thick white foamy cum all over my chest and then leave the room. I'd lie there on this smelly ass queen-size mattress draped across a dark-brown rickety bed tucked off in the corner for what seemed like years at a time, praying to fucking die! I'd ask God, "Why, Lord, why will you not take me? Apparently, you no longer love me. I have exhausted all of my favor with you. Why won't you just allow them to kill me? Why?" These clowns were three complete waste of nuts their daddies should've pulled out and busted each one of their sorry asses onto their bedsheets.

Staci was there from the moment that I escaped and wound up in the Robbins Police Station. The po-pos actually took real good care of me, not like they usually treat young blacks in the Chi and its surrounding suburbs, especially in the south suburbs.

My ride or die chick, Staci, was the very only reason why I eventually came back around and could trust people once again. If it wasn't for my G, my bitch, my ride or die chick, my lovely twins would've never been born because I would never allow anyone, I mean anyone, back into my inner circle! My sister saved my life. I felt worthless. All I wanted to do was just roll up into a big ball and die. These three trifling bastards had stolen everything from me that made me a woman. I was devastated; I could no longer see any good in anyone anymore. The whole world was cold and black, very black to me, good no longer existed.

CHAPTER NINE

THE TURNING POINT

Life was perfect for both me and Staci. We both were married to a set of the greatest cousins in the whole world, Richard and Reginald Anderson from Harvey-world. They lived on the southeast side of Harvey, a couple blocks east of Halsted Avenue; a lot of Harvey cops resided over in that area. The neighborhood just south of the Nine (159th street) and east of Halsted Avenue. This part of Harvey looks totally different from the rest of Harvey, maybe even a feel of a different state. The cozy little community nestled indiscreetly behind the family dollar on the Nine. Seems as if all the lawns are well manicured over this way.

Staci introduced me to Richard after she felt I was ready to move on from that project situation. My G said I was holding on to the hurt a lil too damn long. She was right, thank God for my G, she was on point with introducing me to my soon-to-be husband!

Staci was dating Richard's favorite cousin, Reginald they were best friends as well as blood-related. They had a bond that was even stronger than titanium, the world's strongest natural minerals! They are the seeds of sisters and raised pretty much as brothers. Hell, we used to refer to them as twins. Where are the twins at, or we be like, "What time are the twins coming over today?" The twins were very respectful. Both of our parents loved the twins, both of them. My mom would call them her sons way before we even started talking about marriage! It's a very beautiful thing when your entire family loves your mate. There is nothing else in the world that could compares to this. Wow!

Reginald had been close to the family for years. As a teen, Reginald used to work at Staci's mother's j-o-b, where she was the lead sectary or receptionist at Kar Kare Auto Spa on the south side of the Chi. Kar Kare was a full-service auto spa where you can get your vehicle towed, repaired, washed, and detailed, or you could even purchase your next vehicle at Kar Kare from Jose. Jose is the owner and lead mechanic. Reginald was the son of one of the mechanic at Kar Kare. Reginald was assigned various odd jobs around the shop. He would run errands, sweep floors, wash cars, take lunch orders, and go pick up lunch for all of Jose's employees. Reginald became very close to Staci's mother because Reg was very respectful and polite. Staci's mom introduced Staci and her soon-to-be husband, Reg. Mr. Anderson stated that Staci was going to be his wife at the very first time he laid his eyes upon her. They dated for three years before they made their engagement official. One year after the announcement of their engagement, Staci graduated from college with a master's degree.

I was married to the finest man to ever sport an army uniform. I was a Proverbs 31 woman. I help nurture my husband's dream. He had my back, and I damn sure had his back! We were tight like Bonnie and Clyde without the crime sprees. I was married to a wonderful God-fearing, family-orientated, and loving man. Let's see, Rich was caramel brown, he stood 6'4" tall, and he weighted a solid 215 pounds. Rich's chest appeared as if he slept in the weight room and ate steroids all day long! No, let's get it straight, he never took steroids at all. I love a man with a great chest! Emm, emm, emmmm! My husband was sexy as hell, very bow-legged, thick as hell, nice ass! A smile, a smile that could charm Hollywood as well as the entire female population! Yes, sir, that's my boo!

Now Reg, he was a bit shorter than Rich. Reg stood at 5'11"; he weighed in at like 185 pounds, definitely a gym body! Reginald was a nice chocolate-brown brother, not too dark but not that light! Reg was too damn short for me but truly a keeper! Perfect match for my sister! Reg was great to her. He was excellent with their kids. The family was in love with him. He could do no wrong, and hell, he wouldn't do any wrong!

The twins were in a terrible auto accident on Blood Highway, the infamous I-57! We both lost our husbands at the same damn time, thanks to a fucking drunk-ass driver. This stupid-ass bastard turned me and Staci's world upside down at the same damn time. We both were devastated; our knights in shining armor are now long gone! Fuck! This asshole definitely changed our lives. My rock, my anchor, my husband, my everything is jus gone!

Even in death, Richard and Reginald took care of their families. Rich left the girl the two hundred thousand dollars apiece in insurance money. My baby left me a one-and-a-half-million-dollar policy. I moved to the Beverly Woods neighborhood area and to a better school for his twins! Reg must have had the same agent because he left Staci and their beautiful girls the same policy to improve their living situation as well! Two good and strong black man!

CHAPTER TEN

BLACK KNIGHT

Everything turned pitch black once I heard the voice at the other end of the phone say the words, "Your husband was involved in a terrible accident. You are needed at the hospital, ASAP!"

On sight of the chaplain, my eyes filled with tears, and I begin yelling, "Noooooooooooooooooo!" My world was fucking over. Now I am twenty-nine years old with two six-year-old children, and I'm a fucking widow! At the top of my lungs, I asked Rich why did he leave me and our beautiful twins. How am I gonna make it on my secretary's salary? Why, why, why? My hurt, quickly turned into anger, frustration, then abandonment! I wondered how I would explain to the girls that Daddy was gone, and he was never to come back home. In sheer disbelief, Rich is gone!

This tall, dark, and hot damn surgical nurse walks in looking like a hood-ass Tyrese Gibson. His voice was so damn deep. Larry's voice was as deep as a man's voice could be without being cartoonish or scary! When he opened his mouth to speak, his words came out like a very melodious song. Trey Songz couldn't sing a better sounding song. He said his name was Lawrence, but his friends called him Larry! Larry begin to comfort me, his melodious voice was very soothing. I jus knew everything was going to be all right whenever Larry opened his mouth. His words would put my soul to complete ease!

Larry's skin was dark as a cup of strong black coffee with no cream or sugar. Larry was black, but he had the smoothest skin you'd ever set your eyes on. Larry was an ex-hustler who appeared to be back on the right track. He claimed to have turned over a new lease, got some gainful employment. Larry's aunt was the director of nurses and pulled a couple strings to get him into the hospital as a custodian who went back to school and worked his way up the nursing rank and file.

Larry stood 6 feet tall; he was a solid 205 pounds. His chest was all big and swollen; a bitch could crawl up on his mountain ass chest and curl up into a ball and sleep for 100 years. A bitch would feel very secure lying on his manly chest while wrapped up in his swollen arms. Larry had a stomach that resembled Michelangelo's statue of *David*. Oh, that's all the fuck that they had in common. Larry was packing! He was very well endowed; Larry was at least eleven inches long and thick! Yeah, a bitch's favorite toy! Damn.

Larry was a perfect gentleman; he was there while I grieved over Rich's death. He allowed me to come along at my own pace. He not only worked at the hospital as a surgical nurse, but he also hustled as a part-time heroin pusher! He'd extend credit to doctors and other nurses until payday and collect that chop! I guess old habits die hard?

CHAPTER ELEVEN

REVENGE

Now back to this bitch fucking my nigga! I'm more pissed of the fact that she would fuck him in my home in my bed more than the act itself of her fucking him! Wait, don't get it twisted, this dirty, dirty muthafucka hurt me as well. He knew that she was my ride or die chick. That dirty bitch knew I'd lay my life down for Staci. The one and only bitch that I'd do that for other than my twins! As I slowly walk toward my walk-in closet with twelve-foot doors that run to the celling, this nigga starts gripping and trying to say she tricked him. "She seduced me into sleeping with her." Staci jus lay there looking at him as if looks could kill, she'd castrate him, stick a knife in his windpipe extra slow, and then let him bleed to death very, very slowly. Staci let him rant and rave while throwing up her under the bus.

Staci politely said, "G, think about it, I'd never cross you in two hundred years. We've been through way, way too much shit to allow this piece of shit break our bond and tear us apart! Hell to the no! No fucking chance." Staci blurts out, "G, this goofy don't even know that I've been recording his simple-minded, thirsty ass for the last three months. Yep, all the phone calls. I've saved all the text messages, and yes, all the damn text messages with him taking off his clothes! Every one of the e-mails with his goofy ass talking about how he wished he had met me first. How he wanted to eat my pussy, how he would pay me to hit these pussy! How the next man who get this pussy is getting such a fucking treat! E-mails with him saying how jealous he was of the next man was gonna get what he'd been hoping to just get a quick smell of this pussy!"

"G, I told him that I'd lay my life down before I'd ever think about crossing my girl, my bitch, my ride or die chick! Then this trifling dirty double-dipping bitch got to talking big shit. Darling, please listen to me. This ratchet bitch just don't want us to be together." Larry went on to say, "Darling, we are a power couple like Jada and Will or Jigga and Beyoncé. That ratchet-ass bitch jus' want yo spot, darling, what you got." Larry proceeded to say with his country-ass drawl, "Darling, she ain't got shit, and she's not gonna be happy 'til you sitting here looking like her sorry ass with nothing."

My head starting spinning, so I just yelled out, "Stop! Shut up! Shut the fuck up! Every goddamn body, jus shut the fuck up! I-I-I-I gotta sort some shit out."

Staci took three steps toward my slightly opened midnight black ten-karat-gold-trimmed solid oak armoire.

I blurted out, "Where the fuck you think you going, bitch?"

Staci kept her calm and her composure unlike Staci's always ready to get it crunked ass.

Staci cracked a smile that only her sophisticated ghetto ass could. Staci began, "I knew his sorry low-life lying ass was gonna try and pull some bullshit like this, so I recorded his dumb ass." G, check this shit out. Staci proceeded over to my armoire. Larry started murmuring some inaudible shit as my G, my bitch, my ride or die chick reached into the doors. Staci said to Larry, "What's that? We can't hear you, slick."

Larry said, "Fuck this, fuck this shit, fuck this bitch, and fuck you too, bitch! I'm muthafucking Larry, and Larry don't have to take none of this bull!"

Larry began walking toward my walk-in closet; I reach for my pearl-handled snub-nosed nickel-plated .38. "No, bitch, no, where are you going? Yo mama is a bitch, and we gonna see what's on this tape right here."

Larry was like, "No need, let me put on my clothes, and I'm out of this muthafucker." Larry slips on his Chicago Bulls black and red warm-up suit, slides on his red and black trimmed number 11 classic looks at Staci, mouths the words fuck you, and turns to me and says I'll be back later to retrieve the rest of my shit. Larry strolls out, head held high up in the air as if he was somewhere that was way beneath his likings, rather snobbish at that. Staci and I laugh as Larry's bruised pride walks out. We say in sync as if we were En Vogue or somebody, "Looser!"

CHAPTER TWELVE

A PLEASANT SURPRISE

Staci grabs her mini camcorder; we are watching the playback over the petite playback screen. As we're squinting, I say, "Let's hook it up to the flat screen." As Staci fumbles around with them damn cords, I began to strip my bedding. "Ewh," I say to Staci. I'm gonna burn this damn sheet set. I'd never be able to sleep under that shit again. Just the fucking nerve of his old dirty ass. Staci finally finish hooking up her camcorder to my TV. I think she stalled on purpose so that she wouldn't have to help strip my bed, but that's okay, she's gonna help me flip that bitch over, I betcha!

"Uh, bitch, wait, let me lock up and make a phone call to CPD before we watch this tape." I know it's gonna be funny as hell. I grab my cell phone as I escape down the stairs leading to the kitchen to ensure that trifling-ass Larry left my crib. I make it to my kitchen door as him and his black Escalade is pulling out of my damn driveway. Whew, good ridings to a sorry excuse for a man. I made an important phone call to my friend as I locked my door. I grabbed two bottles of chilled pinot wine from my wine chiller and scurried on back up the stairs.

We sat down in front of my TV on my big-ass comfy recliners that are strategically placed in my room near my pretty sixty-inch TV. The audio is muttered like a muthafucker, straight distorted; however, if you turn up the surround sound and be quiet, you can barely make out what is being said by this simple-minded muthafucka. We notice Larry's irritable behavior as Staci tells Larry that she was going to get a couple of glasses from the kitchen. Larry was in the closet on his knees constantly looking over his shoulder as if he was expecting someone to bust him like a twelve-year-old looking at his daddy's pinup magazines. Just plain weird in nature. We get up and stroll over to my walk-in closet. At first glance, we see nothing. We drop down to our knees so that we are at Larry's height when he was in here, acting like a scared chicken on slaughter day. Bam, there we go. There's a dark-colored duffel bag and another one. Wait, there's one more bag, totaling there nice-size duffel bags—a black one, a brown one, and a dark-green one. We drag these heavy-ass duffel bags over to my California king-size bed. Before we even open the black bag, we can smell it reeking of the bomb as Keesha, this nigga, was using my crib as his muthafucking safe house. This dirty-ass bastard, my kids, my precious twins, could've found his stash! Oooh, oh, he's gonna get, oh, he's gonna get it! I open this duffel, and Staci opens up the green duffel. Staci finds black plastic wrapped around several packages, maybe twenty or so packages. I'm stunned that he have the audacity to bring that shit into my twin's home. I begin to cry, just thinking of all of the negative outcomes that could've been, and my babies were here in this drug heaven. I pull myself tighter with Staci's help and a glass or three of wine. We take a very deep breath and open up the brown bag. We refocus our eyes, and we could not believe what we were seeing. Staci and I reached in at the same time and pulled out a bundle apiece. We fanned through our bundles as if we drew stick figures on the corners and was trying to animate the figures as we all did way back in middle school. Each bundle was wrapped with those big-ass rubber bands that the mailman would hold his letters together. There were twenty bundles of one hundred $100 bills, fifty bundles of one hundred $50 bills, twenty-five bundles of one hundred $20, and fifty-five bundles of one hundred $10. We just inherited a little over a half of a million, just enough to hold me and my babies off until I graduate with my doctorate degree.

We both knew several ballers in the dark world who we could trust and pass along them bricks. They would be very happy to cop these bricks at fifteen racks apiece so they can turn a great profit. These fellas ain't ask any questions. We all know that Staci and I are not about that life! That's another three hundred K Staci and I can use toward our children's future. Hey, we jus might make it after all.

CHAPTER THIRTEEN

THE TRAFFIC STOP

Larry flew out of my driveway as if he was in Doc Brown's DeLorean. So not a way to treat an Escalade. Hey, it's his Cadillac, so let him tear it up. He was bumping NWA's classic "Fuck tha Police." On a regular, Larry would roll around with his twin pearl-handled chrome-plated .45-caliber Smith & Wesson semiautomatic handguns. Once he turned off 103rd onto Western Avenue, Larry was spotted by CPD's drug and gang task force, and they popped on their lights. Over the loudspeaker, the cop braked out, "Driver, pull over! Driver, pull over, pull the fuck over!" Chicago Police Department was known to display a little more aggression when pulling over drivers, that let's say did not have natural blue eyes and blond hair. It was like a muthafuckin' scene from one of Martin Scorsese's action-packed mob movies. Red and blue police lights dancing in the midnight sky. CPD asked Larry's dumb ass to turn off his motor and to get out of his vehicle. Larry leaned over toward the passenger seat to open up the glove box and pulled something shiny out of it. CPD opened fire on Larry, riddling his SUV with bullet, leaving quarter-size holes into the once-pretty black Escalade. Larry was hit with at least twenty bullets once Chicago stopped shooting.

According to the local nine o'clock news, an anonymous caller phoned in a very valuable tip to their lead anchor reporter. The same anchor reporter who received a tip that led to the arrest and permanent removal from Chicago streets, a local dirty-ass drug dealer, and the seizure of ten thousand dollars in cold hard cash and over one hundred thousand dollars in street value of that Keesha!

One of these days, these silly-ass bastards and dumb-ass bitches will learn not to fuck with me and my bitch, my G, my ride or die chick.

ACKNOWLEDGEMENTS

First and foremost I'd like to thank GOD, my Lord and savior for allowing me to transfer my thoughts to words on paper. Secondly, I'd like to thank my fellow co-worker Ms. Pamela R. Maloney who encouraged me to begin writing. Last, but most defiantly I'd like to thank My BFF, or My Ride or Die Chick, for being whom she Is, and always will be, Ms. Ronita Hurt. Thank You all, there are way too many more people that deserve thanks, but I can't fit you all in, just know that You are in my heart. GOD Bless You all!